I Am Somebody

Words by Laura Greene

Pictures by Gerald Cross

 CHILDRENS PRESS, CHICAGO

3 4 5 6 7 8 9 10 11 12 R 86 85 84 83

Library of Congress Cataloging in Publication Data

Greene, Laura.
I am somebody.

SUMMARY: Two friends who feel "like a nobody" on
their baseball teams discuss what does make them feel
important and decide that being themselves is what
really matters.
[1. Self-acceptance—Fiction.   2. Baseball—
Fiction] I. Cross, Gerald. II. Title.
PZ7.G8413Iac   [E]   79-22288
ISBN 0-516-01476-5

I Am Somebody

Nathan was the first one at the baseball playing field. He leaned his bike against a tree and sat on the grass, waiting. He was on the Expos, a minor league team. Nathan knew he would never be good enough for the majors. Eddie was sure to make the majors next year. Eddie was the kind of player that everyone clapped and cheered for, the kind of player everyone liked.

Nathan dreamed about being the starting pitcher and winning the game for his team. As the coach and the other players began arriving, Nathan continued dreaming.

The boys broke up into groups of two and started practicing. No one asked Nathan to join in. He watched the boys playing catch. They were having a good time. He wanted to play catch too, but no one asked him. I guess I'm not even good enough for the minors, he thought.

Nathan looked at his bike. It was old and rusty. The basket was bent. Eddie had a new bike. It had a mirror, reflectors, and a gauge that showed how many miles he pedaled. Nathan's bike had belonged to his cousin. The stickers, which were once so bright, were faded and torn. No one had bothered to take them off.

"You don't need a new bike," his father had said. "This one is good enough."

Eddie not only had a good bike, but Eddie was the best pitcher on the Expos.

Nathan tried to think what he was good in, but he couldn't. He wasn't good in anything that other people thought important.

After a while the coach called the team together. He picked the players for the first two innings, but he did not choose Nathan. Why should he, thought Nathan. I'm not any good, anyway.

"You may play in the third inning," said the coach.

Nathan nodded and sat down to watch the game. He wished he were home. If he were home, he would be working on his collection.

When it was finally his turn to bat, the pitcher walked him to first base. It was better than striking out. He hoped he could make it all the way home on other people's hits. The next player struck out, but the third player hit a grounder. Nathan ran as fast as he could, but it wasn't fast enough. He was out at second. I wish I were a better runner, he thought as he slowly walked back to the bleachers.

In the field, Nathan saw the ball coming directly toward him. He was sure he had it. He wanted to have it, but it slipped out of his glove.

The other kids started yelling at him. Didn't they know he was trying? He picked up the ball and threw it toward first base. It went way beyond the first baseman. Now the team was really angry with him. They were losing, and it was his fault.

The Royals were ahead by seven runs as the Expos moved in to bat. Nathan wished he could do something.

The Royals put in a new pitcher, Brian Ring. Nathan liked Brian. He sat next to him in school. Brian struck out the first batter. Nathan watched as Brian continued to pitch. His pitches were wild now. He wasn't doing very well. In fact, Brian began walking everyone. One by one the runs were walked in.

Then a second player struck out. It was Eddie's turn now. The score was tied, the bases loaded. All eyes were on Eddie. Nathan really admired him. He was glad he was on Eddie's team.

Brian took a long time getting ready to throw the first ball. At last he threw it. Eddie hit the ball with a loud crack. It was a home run. Nathan cheered along with his teammates. With that one hit, Eddie put his team ahead by four runs. It would be hard for the Royals to catch up.

Although Brian struck out the next batter, the Expos felt like winners as they moved onto the field. Eddie was their pitcher. The whole team was counting on him as the game moved into the bottom half of the last inning.

Eddie easily struck out the first two batters. Then Brian Ring came up to bat. Slowly Eddie wound up. Brian swung and connected. Eddie reached up high and caught the ball. The game was over. The Expos won.

The team ran over to congratulate Eddie. Nathan was elbowed out of the way.

Nathan was glad his team won, but he didn't feel a part of them. He walked away from his teammates, got on his bike and started pedaling home through the park.

Soon Brian pedaled along side of him. Nathan could see he felt bad, so he said, "At least you hit one."

Brian nodded. He looked at Nathan, then at his bike. "Hey, I like those stickers," he said.

"Thanks," answered Nathan, and then he added, "Don't you hate it when people yell at you when you make a mistake?"

"It's awful," agreed Brian. "Today I felt like a nobody. My team lost because of me."

"My team won, and it wasn't because of me!" grinned Nathan.

The two boys laughed.

"Want to come to my house to see my collection?" asked Nathan.

"Sure," said Brian.

The two boys pedaled to Nathan's house. Nathan pulled a box out from under his bed.

"That's some box," said Brian.

"Thanks," said Nathan. "I made it. I like working on my collection. I'm better at it than baseball."

"I'm not much good at baseball either," said Brian, "but I like to play."

"Me too, but I wish I were as good as Eddie."

"Eddie practices a lot," said Brian.

"Even if I practiced, I wouldn't be as good a player as Eddie," said Nathan.

"Neither would I," agreed Brian, "but who says we have to be? Other things are important too."

Nathan nodded, then carefully opened his collection box. "I collect feathers," he said. "I find them in the woods, at the zoo, and in the park. Sometimes I buy them, and sometimes my aunt sends me some. When I find a feather, I try to discover what kind of bird lost it. Then I read about the bird."

"You must know a lot about birds."

"I guess so," said Nathan. "I spend a lot of time at it."

"Why?"

"I like it, and I'm good at it."

"How do you know you're good? Did someone tell you?" asked Brian.

"No one has to tell me. When I do something well, I know it. I hum inside. It's a nice feeling. I feel like somebody."

"I get that feeling too, sometimes," said Brian.

"I wish baseball gave me that feeling, but it doesn't. Sometimes I wish I were Eddie," said Nathan.

"I'm glad you're not, and just because Eddie's good at baseball doesn't mean you have to be," said Brian.

"I suppose not. I'm good at some things, but not others. That's just me, and being me is what really matters."

E
G   Greene, Laura
    JAN 25.1985   I am somebody

DATE D

E
G   Greene, Laura
    JAN 25.1985   I am somebody

DATE	BORROWER'S NAME	
AUG 14.1985	Brian Keenn	
MAY 23.1986	Kate	
9/56	Ky	SEP. 29.1986
.S.		
	7 190	

DISCARD